Freddie Fernortner

FEARLESS FIRST GRADER ©

Freddie   Darla   Chipper   Mr. Chewy

THE BIG BOX FORT
BY JOHNATHAN RAND

An AudioCraft Publishing, Inc. book

Freddie Fernortner, Fearless First Grader
#5: The Big Box Fort
ISBN 1-893699-83-8

Illustrations by Cartoon Studios, Battle Creek, Michigan

Visit www.freddiefernortner.com

Printed in USA

First Printing - October 2005

THE
BIG
BOX
FORT

1

Have you ever wanted to build a really big fort? One that you and your friends could play in, all day?

Well, Freddie, Chipper, and Darla thought that it would be a lot of fun . . . and they decided to do it.

Darla's mother and father bought a new refrigerator, and it came in a big box. Darla's father was going to throw the big box away with the trash, but the three first graders had other plans.

First, Darla asked her dad if she could have the box. When her father said 'yes,' she was very excited. She ran across the street where Freddie, Chipper, and Mr. Chewy waited on Freddie's porch. Mr. Chewy was chewing on a wad of gum, blowing a bubble.

"My dad said yes!" Darla said excitedly.

"That's cool!" Chipper said. He spread his arms wide. "Let's build a super-giant fort!"

"Yeah!" Freddie agreed. "Big enough for all three of us!"

The three first graders, followed by Mr. Chewy, walked across the street to Darla's house. The big box was in the garage.

"Gee, it's bigger than we are," Chipper said. "How are we going to move it?"

"Well, it's bigger than we are, that's for sure," Freddie said, "but it's made out of cardboard. It shouldn't be too heavy."

Freddie was right. The box was big, but it wasn't very heavy. But, because of its size, they couldn't pick it up.

"Let's just drag it across the street and into my back yard," Freddie said.

They tipped the box over. Then, they each grabbed hold of it and pulled, dragging it out of the garage. All the while, Mr. Chewy watched and chewed his bubble gum.

After struggling for a few minutes, they were able to drag the big box across the street and into Freddie's back yard.

"We'll leave it on its side and make a door," Freddie said.

"What about the ends?" Chipper asked. They flopped open and closed.

"My dad has some really sticky tape in the garage," Freddie said. "We can tape the ends closed so that no light can get in."

"First, let's go inside," Darla said, "and see if the three of us can fit."

That seemed like a good idea, so

Freddie, Chipper, and Darla scrambled inside, through the open ends. Mr. Chewy was quick to follow.

"There's just barely enough room for us," Chipper said. "It's too bad the box isn't bigger."

They climbed out of the box.

Just then, Freddie's mom opened up the back door.

"Freddie," she called, "lunchtime."

"Okay, Mom," Freddie called back. Then he turned to Darla and Chipper. "Let's meet back here after lunch. Then, we'll get to work on our fort."

Chipper and Darla went home.

After lunch, Freddie and Mr. Chewy went into the garage and found his dad's tape. It was silver-colored and very sticky. He carried it into the back yard and waited for his friends.

Soon, Chipper showed up. He and Freddie and Mr. Chewy waited for Darla.

But, she didn't show up.

They waited some more.

"Maybe she can't come over," Chipper said.

Just then, the front door of Darla's house opened and Darla appeared. She saw Freddie and Chipper, and she waved frantically.

"You guys!" she shouted. "You're not going to believe it!"

"What?" Freddie asked, but Darla was already on the move, running toward them. She stopped at the street, looked both ways, and then continued running. By the time she arrived in Freddie's back yard, she was out of breath.

"What's going on?" Chipper asked. "Why are you so excited?"

"Wait until I tell you," Darla gasped. "You're not going to believe it!"

2

"When I told my mom what we were doing," Darla explained, "she told me that our neighbor on the other side of our back yard has a bunch of boxes!"

Freddie's eyes grew wide.

Chipper's eyes grew even wider.

"Really?" Freddie asked.

Darla nodded. "I went and looked. He has a whole bunch of big boxes. He said he was going to throw them away!"

"Throw them away?!?!" Chipper gasped.

"Not anymore," Darla said. "I asked him if we could have them for our fort, and he said yes!"

"That's so cool!" Freddie exclaimed. "Let's go get them right now!"

And so, Freddie, Chipper, Darla, and Mr. Chewy went across the street and into Darla's back yard. They went to her neighbor's yard. Sure enough, there was a bunch of very large boxes next to the house.

"Wow!" Chipper said. "We hit the jackpot!"

"We're going to be able to build a super-huge fort!" Freddie said.

"It'll be the biggest fort in the world!" Darla exclaimed.

It took them almost an hour, but the

three finally dragged all of the boxes to
Freddie's back yard.

And they got to work.

They taped boxes together and cut doors on the inside, so each box was a different room.

And the fort got bigger.

And bigger.

And sometimes, when you work really hard, an idea might come to you without warning.

And that's what happened to Freddie Fernortner, Fearless First Grader.

It was a big idea.

A *good* idea.

In fact, his idea was so good, he dropped the tape he was working with.

"That's it!" he said, stepping back and looking at the fort.

"What?" Chipper said loudly, from somewhere inside the fort.

"What, Freddie?" Darla asked, poking her head through a window cut out of the side of a box.

"I know how we can make our fort even bigger!" Freddie exclaimed.

Darla scrambled out of the fort, and Chipper followed. Mr. Chewy stood in the doorway, chewing bubble gum and blowing a bubble.

What do you think Freddie's good idea was?

Chipper and Darla were about to find out.

3

"Let's build a second story!" Freddie said excitedly.

Chipper looked confused. "What do you mean?" he asked.

"I mean, let's put boxes on top of our fort!" Freddie said. "We can make our fort have two floors!"

"Oh, I know what you mean!" Darla blurted. "Like our house! We have stairs that go up to my bedroom!"

"Exactly!" Freddie said. "Only we won't need stairs. All we'll need is a short ladder or something to stand on."

"We can use a milk crate!" Chipper said. "We have some in our garage!"

"Perfect!" Freddie said.

The three first graders were more excited than ever, and they got to work building a second floor on their fort. Soon the fort was attracting attention. Other kids from the neighborhood stopped to watch for a few minutes. Cars on the street slowed to see the big fort in Freddie's back yard.

And, just as you can imagine, it looked very, very cool.

But something was about to happen that wasn't very cool.

In fact, what was about to happen was very, very scary.

4

After they had finished the second story, the three stood in the yard, looking at the fort they had built.

"This is great!" Freddie said.

"But we still have more boxes left, Freddie," Darla said.

They looked at the boxes that remained in the yard.

Then, they looked at the fort.

Chipper grinned.

Darla smiled.

Freddie smiled, too. He looked at Darla, and then at Chipper. "Are you guys thinking the same thing I'm thinking?" he asked. His smile widened.

"Yeah," Chipper said. "Let's build a *third* story!"

"Yeah!" Darla exclaimed.

Once again, the three got to work. All the while, Mr. Chewy looked on, chewing bubble gum and blowing bubbles. Every once in a while the cat would wander into the fort and look around. Then, he would wander back out, sit down, and watch the three first graders busy at work.

More people stopped by Freddie's back yard to see the huge box fort. Cars stopped on the street, and people got out to look.

Freddie, Chipper, and Darla were

having a lot of fun . . . but it was about to end.

What was about to happen wasn't fun at all.

It happened when Freddie, Chipper, and Darla were on the third story, taping the last box in place.

Suddenly, without warning, a portion of the fort gave way! Darla shrieked, and Chipper screamed. Freddie tried to grab a box, but it was too late.

A part of the fort collapsed, taking the three first graders with it.

5

Everything was dark.

Freddie couldn't see a thing.

Darla couldn't see anything, either.

Chipper was in total darkness.

"Darla! Chipper!" Freddie cried, as he pushed boxes out of his way. "Are you okay?"

"I'm okay," Chipper said. "But there's a box on me!"

"I'm okay, too," Darla said. "But I

can't see a thing!"

They worked hard to free themselves from the boxes that had fallen around them. Soon, they had scrambled out of the mess.

"Wow," Freddie said. "We'll have to be more careful. We could've been hurt."

"That was scary," Darla said.

"I think we can fix it so that it doesn't happen again," Freddie said. "Let's use some pieces of wood to hold up the boxes. Wood is a lot stronger than cardboard."

"Good idea," Chipper agreed, rubbing his head. "I don't want to fall and bump my noodle again."

And so, the three got to work again, this time using some scrap wood they found next to Freddie's garage. They worked hard to rebuild the fort, making it stronger so it wouldn't collapse.

"This is going to be the best box fort in the whole world!" Freddie said while they worked.

"In the whole universe!" Chipper said. "I'll bet nobody has a fort like we do!"

The three first graders worked hard into the afternoon. Still more neighborhood kids stopped by to marvel at the big box fort that was growing in Freddie's back yard. More cars stopped. Even Freddie's mom looked out the window every once in a while.

"My," she said proudly, "Freddie and his friends sure are smart."

Finally, they were finished. The three scrambled out of the fort to look at it.

"Wow," Freddie breathed.

"Oooh," Darla whispered.

"Gee," Chipper said quietly.

The fort was big . . . bigger than

they'd even imagined. It was three stories tall, and it had a single cardboard door that swung open and closed. A few of the boxes had holes cut out for windows.

"We did it!" Freddie exclaimed. "We really did it!"

A noise from the front of the house caught their attention.

Freddie turned.

Chipper turned.

Darla turned.

Mr. Chewy blew a bubble and turned.

"Oh my gosh!" Darla said.

"Whoa!" Chipper said.

"Holy smokes!" Freddie exclaimed.

The three first graders couldn't believe what they were seeing.

6

It was a television camera crew!

There was a big white van from the local television station parked in Freddie's driveway! A pretty lady was carrying a microphone. She was walking toward the three first graders in the back yard. A man followed, and he was carrying a camera!

"That's a very big fort you've built," the pretty lady said. "Would you like to be on TV?"

"You bet!" Freddie said.

"That would be cool!" Chipper exclaimed.

"Yeah!" piped Darla. "We'll be famous!"

The man with the camera began filming. The pretty lady asked questions about the fort. Freddie, Chipper, and Darla took turns answering her. The cameraman even got on his hands and knees and went into the fort with his camera!

"I must say," the pretty lady said, "you three are very smart. Not many kids these days work hard and have so much fun at the same time."

"When are we going to be on TV?" Chipper asked.

"You'll be on the six-o'clock news tonight," she said. "I might even make it our top story."

"The top story?!?!" the three first graders chimed.

After the television news crew left, Freddie, Chipper, and Darla climbed into the fort, followed by Mr. Chewy. They climbed all around, up to the second and third floors.

More neighborhood kids came by, and the three first graders waved to them from inside their big fort.

"We're going to be on television!" they told the other kids. "Tonight, on the news! Be sure to watch us!"

After dinner, everyone gathered at Freddie's to watch the news. The house was packed! Not only were Chipper and Darla there, but their families, too! Even Chipper's older brother came.

When the news came on at six o'clock, Mr. Fernortner turned the volume up so everyone could hear.

Sure enough, the big box fort was the top story! The pretty lady came on TV and talked about it.

Suddenly, there they were! Freddie, Chipper, and Darla, standing proudly in front of their fort. Even Mr. Chewy was on television!

When it was over, everyone was very proud of the three first graders. After all, it isn't every day that you get to be on TV.

Freddie, Chipper, and Darla went outside after the news. Everyone else stayed inside, talking and laughing and drinking lemonade.

"Hey," Darla said. "I've got an idea!"

"What?" Freddie and Chipper asked.

"Remember when we set up the tent in your back yard?" Darla asked. "When we read scary stories after dark, with a flashlight?"

Freddie and Chipper nodded. That had been a lot of fun.

"Well, why not do that in our fort tonight?" Darla suggested. "We can take turns reading scary stories in our fort!"

"Darla, that would be great!" Freddie exclaimed.

"Yeah!" Chipper agreed. "I've got a book of really scary stories from the school library! We can read from it tonight!"

And so, that's what they decided to do. They would wait until it was dark, and then they would all meet in Freddie's back yard. Then, they would go into the fort and take turns reading from Chipper's scary book.

However, they didn't realize that they wouldn't be alone.

Oh, Mr. Chewy would be there, of course.

But something else was also going to be there.

Inside the fort.

Watching.

And for Freddie, Chipper, and Darla, it would be a terrifying experience.

7

Later that evening, just as the sun was going down, Freddie and Mr. Chewy went into the back yard.

A star twinkled above.

Then another.

And another.

A full moon shone brightly, all silvery and blue.

Crickets chirped.

It grew darker.

Soon, Freddie saw Darla's figure in the glow of the street light.

"Freddie?" she called out.

"I'm here," Freddie replied. "In my back yard."

Darla crossed the street and found her way to Freddie's back yard. Here, the big box fort looked like a big, dark, square mountain, faintly aglow by the light of the moon.

"Where's Chipper?" Darla asked.

"He's not here yet," Freddie replied.

No sooner had Freddie said those words, than they saw the beam of a flashlight appear.

"Where are you guys?" Chipper asked.

"Over here," Freddie said.

Chipper found his way to Freddie and Darla. He was carrying a book, and he held it under the flashlight beam.

"*Terrifying Stories to Read Out Loud,*" Freddie said, reading the cover.

"This is going to be so much fun!" Darla said. "Let's go into the fort!"

Chipper aimed the flashlight beam at the door of the fort.

Freddie pushed the door open.

Inside, the fort was very, very dark.

"I'm glad we have a flashlight," Darla said. "It looks sort of spooky."

"There's nothing to be afraid of," Freddie said. "We'll be all by ourselves."

Freddie went inside first, followed by Darla, then Chipper, and, finally, Mr. Chewy. They climbed through several boxes until they were seated in a very dark, small room. The box had two windows, and cool night air drifted in.

"This spot will be perfect," Freddie said, taking a seat in the corner. Chipper sat on one side of him, and Darla sat on the other. Mr. Chewy wandered around a bit, and his claws made a scratching sound on the cardboard. Then, he sat down.

"I'll start," Chipper said, opening up the book.

He began to read.

The story was quite scary, and Darla held Freddie's hand.

But, they weren't afraid, because they knew that it was only a story.

Still, Darla was glad that Freddie and Chipper were there. And Mr. Chewy, too. The cat was sitting next to her, but in the darkness, she couldn't see him. But she patted his head and scratched him behind his ears.

Or, she *thought* that it was Mr. Chewy.

After all . . . it was small and furry . . . just like Mr. Chewy.

Chipper finished reading, and he handed the book to Freddie. "Your turn," he said. Next to Chipper, Mr. Chewy shifted and got to his feet. Darla saw this.

She stared.

Because she was still petting Mr. Chewy with her right hand. She could feel his soft fur beneath her fingers.

But that was impossible . . . because Mr. Chewy had moved, and was now next to Chipper!

And if Mr. Chewy wasn't sitting next to her, just what was?

"Ch-Ch-Chipper," she stammered, pulling her hand away, "sh-sh-shine the l-l-light over h-h-here."

Chipper shined the light next to Darla.

Then he gasped.

Freddie gasped.

Darla screamed.

Sitting next to her wasn't Mr. Chewy.

It wasn't even a cat.

Or a small dog.

It was a skunk!

8

"Run for your lives!" Freddie shrieked.

Chipper wasted no time, and dove out the window. Freddie tried to jump out the other window, but he bumped into Darla. Mr. Chewy ran to the other side of the box, through a door, and vanished.

"Hurry, Freddie, hurry!" Darla exclaimed. "Before he sprays us and we get all stinky!"

Freddie finally dove out a window,

and he turned around to help Darla out. She tumbled to the damp grass.

"Mr. Chewy!" Freddie called out. "Where are you?"

Chipper shined the light all around, and the cat suddenly appeared, walking toward them in the grass.

"I can't believe that!" Chipper said. "We could have been attacked!"

"Skunks don't attack people," Freddie said. "But if he would have sprayed us, we would smell bad for years!"

"I wonder how he got in there," Darla said.

"I don't know," Chipper said, "but I'm not going back in there until he's gone."

"I guess we'll have to wait until tomorrow," Freddie said. "Maybe if we leave him alone, he'll leave."

A shrill voice suddenly pierced the night.

"Chipper!"

"Yeah, Mom?" Chipper shouted back.

"Time to get ready for bed," his mother called.

"Be right there!" Chipper shouted.

"I should go home, too," Darla said.

"Let's meet here in the morning," Freddie said, "and then we'll see if the skunk is still in our fort."

Chipper and Darla agreed.

Would the skunk still be there?

They would have to wait until the next day to find out.

One thing was for sure, though.

Freddie, Chipper, and Darla were in for another day full of surprises.

9

The next morning was cloudy and gray. Freddie, Darla, and Chipper met in Freddie's back yard.

But they didn't get close to the fort.

Not yet, anyway.

After all . . . they didn't know if the skunk was still inside.

"How do we know if it's gone?" Darla asked.

"I don't know," Freddie said. "I hadn't thought of that."

Just then, three third graders appeared around the corner of Freddie's house. Freddie recognized them. They were bigger, and sometimes, they weren't very nice.

"Hey Freddie!" one of the kids said. "We want to see the inside of your fort!"

Freddie shook his head. "You can't go inside," he said.

"Why not?" one of the bigger kids asked.

"Because there's a skunk in there, that's why," Darla said. "He'll make you all smelly."

"Aww, you just don't want us in your fort," one of the kids said.

"No, really," Chipper said. "We saw a skunk in there last night. He might still be there."

"Well, why don't you let us go and look for ourselves?" one of the kids said.

"I don't think that's a good idea," Freddie said. "If he sprays you, you're going to smell really, really bad."

The three kids approached.

"I think you're just making it up," one kid said. "I don't think there's a skunk in there. You're just trying to keep us out of your fort."

"No, really, guys," Freddie said. "We really *did* see a skunk in there last night. He might still be there."

"Then you wouldn't mind if we went inside and checked it out, would you?" the kid said. "Come on, guys. Let's go see for ourselves."

The three third graders walked past the three first graders.

"You're going to be sorry," Darla said.

"If that skunk is in there, you're going to be in a lot of trouble."

"You're making it up," one of the kids said, as he reached the door of the fort. Then, he pushed the cardboard door open and went inside.

His two friends followed him.

"I hope that skunk is gone," Freddie said.

"I hope it's still there," Darla said angrily. "It would serve them right."

They could hear the three third graders inside the fort.

"This is cool!"

"Neat!"

"Wow!"

"What a cool fort!"

And then:

"Aaaahhhhhhh!"

"Oh no!"

"Run! Run! Run!"

There were all sorts of different sounds now. Sounds of scratching on cardboard, frantic thrashing, and bumping.

"Oh no!" Freddie said. "The skunk! It's still in our fort!"

It was true.

The skunk was still in the fort.

So were the three bigger kids.

But Freddie, Chipper, and Darla couldn't believe what happened next.

10

One of the third graders tried to dive out one of the windows, but he was too big. Instead of getting stuck, however, the cardboard ripped, creating a huge hole! The kid tumbled outside, holding his nose. His two friends followed.

"Skunk!" one of them shouted. "There's a skunk in there!"

They took off running, vanishing around the front of Freddie's house.

"Well, at least we know where the skunk is," Freddie said.

"How are we going to get him out of there?" Chipper asked.

"Yeah," Darla said. "We worked really hard on our fort, and now we can't go inside. Not until the skunk is gone."

"How do you get rid of a skunk?" Chipper asked.

Freddie scratched his head. "I don't know," he said. "I've never had to kick out a skunk before."

"Can we trap him in a box?" Darla asked.

Freddie shook his head. "We could try, but he'd probably spray skunky stuff all over us," he said.

"We could just wait," Chipper said. "He's bound to leave sometime."

"But what if he likes it in there?"

Darla said. "What if he decides to make our fort his home?"

"I guess I hadn't thought of that," Freddie said. "If he likes it in there, and decides to stay, we'll never be able to go into our fort again."

The three first graders thought really hard. Mr. Chewy sat nearby, chewing his gum and blowing bubbles.

"What do skunks like to eat?" Chipper asked. "Maybe we could lure him out with some food."

"I don't know what they eat," Freddie replied.

"They probably like smelly stuff," Darla suggested.

"Yeah," Chipper said. "They probably eat things that smell bad. That's why they're so stinky."

"There's got to be a way to get him

out of there," Freddie said. "Maybe we should try to think about what he doesn't like."

"What do you mean?" Darla asked.

"Well," Freddie said, "if you were a skunk, what wouldn't you like?"

"I don't know," Darla said with a shrug. "I'm not a skunk."

Just then, Chipper's eyes lit up.

"I've got it!" he exclaimed. "I know what the skunk doesn't like!"

"What?" Freddie asked.

"My brother's music!" Chipper replied. "Nobody likes it! It's terrible! Sometimes, he plays it really loud in his bedroom, and my mom and dad get really mad. My dad says that there's no creature on the planet that could like that kind of music!"

"What kind of music is it?" Darla

asked.

"I don't know," Chipper said, shaking his head. "But it's really, really bad. I can't stand it."

"And neither will the skunk!" Freddie exclaimed.

"Exactly!" Chipper said. "My brother is gone all day. I'll go get his stereo, and we can set it by the door of the fort and play the music really loud. That'll drive the skunk crazy, and maybe he'll leave!"

It was a daring plan, that was for sure.

But would it work?

Would they be able to get the skunk to leave their fort by playing really bad music?

They were about to find out.

11

Chipper's brother's radio was so big that he had to use his wagon to haul it across the street to Freddie's back yard.

"That thing must weigh a ton!" Freddie said, as Chipper pulled the wagon into the back yard.

"I don't know why they make them so big," Chipper said. "Maybe that's why it's so loud."

Carefully, Freddie and Chipper lifted the radio out of the wagon and carried it to the front door of the fort. Darla and Mr. Chewy looked on.

"Be careful," Darla said. "That smelly skunk might be waiting for you, right on the other side of the door."

Freddie slowly pushed open the cardboard door.

He peered inside.

"He's not here," he said. "But he could be anywhere inside. How do you work this thing, Chipper?"

Chipper fiddled with some knobs. Suddenly, loud, thumping music started playing. A singer started singing, but the three first graders couldn't understand what he was saying.

Darla put her hands over her ears. "That's terrible," she said.

"I know," Chipper agreed. "But my brother really likes it."

Even Mr. Chewy put his paws over his ears. He couldn't stand the music, either.

Chipper found the volume button and turned the music up even louder.

And louder.

Louder still.

"Now what?" Darla shouted over the music. She still had her hands over her ears.

"Now, we wait!" Chipper shouted back. "Let's hope it works!"

The three first graders moved back from the big box fort. They wanted to stand clear in case the skunk came out, and they also wanted to get away from the loud, screeching music.

"Your brother is going to rot his brains listening to that stuff," Freddie said.

"He already has," Chipper said.

"Well, I hope that skunk comes out soon," Darla said. "Sooner or later, everybody in the neighborhood is going to be mad at us."

"Let's just hope it works," Freddie said.

Just then, they caught a movement inside the open door of the fort.

"Look!" Freddie said, pointing.

While they watched, the skunk came out the front door of the fort! It was on its hind legs, and its front legs were covering its ears. The animal looked dizzy, like he was about to go crazy.

"It worked!" Chipper said. "It really worked! The skunk couldn't stand the music, and now he's leaving!"

They watched as the skunk wobbled away, shaking its head from side to side.

"Chipper, you're a genius!" Freddie said.

"Yeah," Darla said. "That sure was smart thinking, Chipper."

Suddenly, Freddie's mother appeared at the kitchen window. "Freddie!" she exclaimed. "Turn down that awful music this instant!"

"Sorry, Mom," Freddie said, and he raced to turn down the radio. "We were just trying to get a skunk out of our fort."

"Well, turn it off," his mother demanded. "That's the worst-sounding music I've ever heard in my life!"

Freddie shut off the radio.

"That's much better," Darla said.

"Help me put it back in the wagon, Freddie," Chipper said. "Then, I'll take it back home."

Freddie and Chipper lifted it up and

put it into the red wagon.

"Do you need help getting it back into your brother's room?" Freddie asked.

"No," Chipper replied. "I'll just drag it in. My brother won't even know that it was missing."

Chipper was gone for a few minutes, and then returned without the wagon.

"Now that the skunk is gone, we can play in our fort all day," Freddie said, "as soon as we fix the hole that those three kids made."

The three scrambled into the fort, followed by Mr. Chewy . . . completely unaware of the dark, dangerous storm clouds that were quickly headed their way.

12

It hadn't taken them long to fix the hole created by the three bigger kids. Freddie used a lot of tape and soon, the fort was as good as new.

Freddie, Chipper, and Darla talked about how they could make the fort even better.

"We could put in glass windows!" Chipper offered.

"That's a good idea, Chipper," Freddie said, "but it would cost money."

"Maybe we could make a slide," Darla said. "You know . . . from the top of the fort to the ground. That would be a lot of fun!"

Freddie and Chipper agreed. A slide would be a blast.

"Wait a minute," Freddie said, looking around. "What was that?"

"What was what?" Chipper asked.

"Did you guys hear anything?"

The three first graders were silent for a moment. Even Mr. Chewy stopped chewing his bubble gum.

"I didn't hear anything, Freddie," Darla said.

"Me neither," Chipper said. "What did you hear?"

"It was a rumbling sound," Freddie

said. "But it was probably just a big truck on the highway."

They continued talking, thinking up ideas, and having fun. Mr. Chewy kept chewing his gum and blowing bubbles.

And they had no idea that a terrible thunderstorm was moving closer.

And closer.

And closer still.

Suddenly, a loud rumble shook the ground, shaking the fort and causing it to tremble. Freddie leaned over and peered out a window.

"A storm is coming!" he exclaimed. "The sky is super-dark!"

Chipper and Darla peeked over his shoulder. Sure enough, the sky was filled with bruised, swollen storm clouds.

Then, it started to rain.

"This is great!" Freddie exclaimed. "Our first storm in our new fort! And we're inside where it's warm and dry!"

The rain began to patter on the roof above them. The wind picked up, and the entire fort shook.

"I'm glad we're in our fort," Darla said, "and not in a tent. The wind would blow the tent away!"

"Yeah," Chipper said. "But our fort is tough. We can stay here until it passes."

And that's what they tried to do.

Freddie, Chipper, and Darla sat inside the big box fort, thinking that they were as snug as a bug beneath a rug.

Until a drip of water landed on Freddie's head.

And another.

Then, a drop of water landed on Chipper's head. And on Mr. Chewy's head.

"Hey," Chipper said. He looked up. "I think our fort has sprung a leak."

Soon, trickles of water began coming in, but the storm showed no signs of letting up.

And there was one very important thing that the three first graders hadn't thought about.

When cardboard gets wet, it softens.

It weakens.

It soaks up water, and gets heavier.

And heavier.

"Uh-oh," Darla said, as she looked up.

Chipper and Freddie looked up.

Above them, the cardboard roof was sagging.

Water was trickling in even faster than before.

"I think we've got problems," Freddie said. "I think we should—"

Freddie never got the chance to finish his sentence. Without warning, the entire box fort collapsed, burying Freddie, Chipper, Darla, and Mr. Chewy inside.

13

Everything happened so fast that no one even had a chance to scream or cry out. One moment, Freddie, Chipper, Darla, and Mr. Chewy were seated on the floor . . . and the next, the entire box fort had collapsed on top of them.

Water poured in. Cold, wet cardboard pushed the three first graders to the ground. Mr. Chewy let out a loud *meow!*

And everything was dark.

Dark . . . and wet.

"Darla! Chipper!" Freddie cried. But his words were muffled, and he sounded like he was far away.

"I'm right here!" Chipper shouted, but his voice, too, sounded a long way off.

"I'm soaked!" Darla said from somewhere. "I'm soaked, and I can't move!"

Mr. Chewy meowed even louder.

"Mr. Chewy!" Freddie called. "It's going to be all right, buddy! You're going to be okay!"

Rain continued to pour. The wind kept blowing.

"Try and push some of the boxes away," Freddie said loudly. "If we can push them off, we can get out!"

Thunder cracked in the sky above. The wind bent the trees.

And the three first graders were very, very scared.

After some struggling, Freddie was able to push some of the cardboard away from him. It was hard, because the cardboard had soaked up the rain, making it heavy and soggy.

Suddenly, Mr. Chewy appeared from beneath one of the soggy pieces of cardboard.

"Mr. Chewy!" Freddie shouted. "Boy, am I glad to see you!"

Mr. Chewy shook, and water went everywhere. Then he took off running toward Freddie's house.

He scrambled to his feet. Rain continued to pour down, and Freddie started peeling cardboard away from the pile in a frantic search for Chipper and Darla.

"Chipper! Darla!" he shouted above the wind and rain. "Where are you?!?!"

"I'm right here!" Darla shouted back, but it was hard to know exactly where she was. He reached down to grab a small hunk of cardboard, and pulled.

"Ow!" Chipper shrieked. "That's my ear!"

"Chipper!" Freddie shouted, and he pulled part of the box away. Chipper scrambled up. He was muddy, but unhurt.

"Darla!" Freddie called out.

"I'm right here, Freddie," Darla called back. It sounded like she was very close to them, but she was buried beneath wet, heavy cardboard.

"Just start pulling the cardboard up!" Freddie said to Chipper. "She's here somewhere!"

Lightning flashed in the sky above,

and thunder rumbled as the two first graders worked to find their friend.

Suddenly, Darla's arm appeared. Freddie grasped her hand and pulled, and Darla finally struggled to her feet.

"What a bummer," Chipper said, as he looked around. Their fort, which once had been three stories tall, was in ruins in the yard.

"Come on," Freddie said. "Let's go into my garage and get out of the rain."

The three first graders ran across the yard, through puddles that had formed in the grass. Freddie opened the back door of the garage and they went inside . . . where his mother stood.

"Freddie Fernortner!" she exclaimed. "I thought you had enough common sense to come in out of the rain!"

"We got trapped in our fort, Mrs. Fernortner," Chipper explained. "The whole thing caved in on us!"

"It was very scary," Darla said. "Freddie saved my life, I think."

"Well, you stay here, and I'll bring some towels," Mrs. Fernortner said. "When it stops thundering and lightning, Chipper and Darla can go home and get some dry clothes."

And so, that was the end of the big box fort. Freddie, Chipper, and Darla spent the next day cleaning up all of the cardboard. They put it in a big pile near the curb, so it would be picked up when the garbage truck came by.

"Well," Darla said, as the three looked at the big pile of soggy cardboard. "What next?"

"Yeah," Chipper said. "We've done

some pretty cool things."

"Like the flying bike," Freddie said.

"And hunting for super-scary night thingys," Darla offered.

"Don't forget about the haunted house," Chipper said. "That was fun."

"And so was our dog walking service," Darla said. "What are we going to do now?"

None of them had any ideas.

Yet.

Until Freddie looked up into a tree and saw something.

At first, he didn't know what it was.

Then, when he realized what he was looking at, he gasped.

Then he pointed.

"Look!" he shouted in excitement. "Look what's in the tree!"

Chipper looked up.

Darla looked, too. "Oh, my!" she said.

In the tree was a beautiful, colorful kite. It had a long tail made of rags that were tied together. The tail was wrapped around the branch.

"Someone lost it during the storm!" Freddie said. "Let's get it down!"

"But Freddie," Darla said, "it's caught in the tree. How are we going to get it?"

"Oh, we'll find a way," Freddie said with a smile.

Chipper covered his face with his hands. "I was afraid you were going to say that," he said.

"Hey, it's only a kite," Freddie said. "What could possibly go wrong?"

"I don't know," Darla said, shaking her head. "But I bet we're about to find out."

Darla was right. The three first

graders, and Mr. Chewy, too, were about to have one of their scariest adventures they've ever had.

They just didn't know it, yet.

NEXT:
FREDDIE FERNORTNER,
FEARLESS FIRST GRADER

BOOK SIX:

MR. CHEWY'S BIG
ADVENTURE

CONTINUE ON TO READ
THE FIRST TWO CHAPTERS
FOR FREE!

1

"I've got an idea!" Freddie Fernortner said to his two friends, Chipper and Darla.

"Oh, brother," Darla said. "Here we go again."

"Are we going to get into trouble?" Chipper asked.

Freddie shook his head. "Not this time," he said.

However, when Freddie Fernortner

said that they wouldn't get into trouble, they usually did.

You see, although Freddie was very smart, he was also very curious . . . and very brave. Once, he and his friends built a flying bicycle. Another time, they visited a haunted house. They even built a giant fort out of old boxes!

One thing was for sure: Freddie and his friends, along with his cat, Mr. Chewy, always had a lot of fun. Mr. Chewy got his name because he likes to chew bubble gum and blow bubbles . . . which was exactly what the cat was doing when Freddie spotted something stuck in a tree.

"Look," Freddie said, pointing. Darla and Chipper turned.

In a tree, not far away, was a kite. It

was a big kite, too, and it was very colorful. Its tail was made of rags that had been tied together. A storm had passed through earlier in the day, and Freddie thought that someone must have been flying the kite when the string broke.

"That's cool!" Chipper said. "It's the biggest kite I've ever seen in my life!"

Chipper was right. The kite was very big.

"It's pretty," Darla said.

"I'll bet we could get it down," Freddie said.

"But Freddie," Darla said, "how are we going to get it? It's stuck in the tree."

"I can climb up," Freddie said. "It's not very high."

Chipper scratched his head. "I don't

know, Freddie," he said. "What happens if you fall?"

"I won't fall," Freddie said. "The kite is stuck on the lowest branch. I could climb up and reach the branch and grab the kite. But I'll need your help."

Not far away, Mr. Chewy sat in the grass, chewing gum. He blew a bubble and it popped. Then, he continued chewing.

"Come on," Freddie said, and the three first graders walked to the tree. Above, the colorful kite fluttered in the breeze.

"How are you going to climb up?" Chipper asked. "There aren't any branches to grab hold of."

"Simple," Freddie said. "You stand next to the tree, Chipper. I'll climb onto your shoulders and reach the branch. Then, I'll climb out and untie the kite."

Darla shook her head. "I don't think it's a good idea, Freddie," she said.

Mr. Chewy, who had followed the three first graders, sat in the grass and blew a bubble.

"Don't worry," Freddie said. "I'll be careful."

Chipper backed up to the tree. In no time at all, Freddie had scrambled to his friends' shoulders. Then, he reached up and grabbed the branch.

"See?" Freddie said, as he swung his legs up over the branch. "This is easy!"

But as he climbed farther out onto the limb, it began to bend.

"I hope the branch doesn't break,"

Chipper said.

"I can't bear to watch," Darla said, covering her eyes with her hands.

"I know!" Freddie said. "Mr. Chewy! Climb up here and help me get the kite!"

Mr. Chewy scampered to the tree and climbed up the trunk. After all, the cat was an expert at climbing trees.

"That's it!" Freddie said, as the cat made his way along the branch. "Climb out past me, and see if you can get the kite unstuck!"

Mr. Chewy seemed to understand, and he climbed past Freddie, walking cautiously along the limb.

On the ground, Chipper watched. Darla peeked through her fingers.

Mr. Chewy approached the kite's

tangled tail.

"Good cat!" Freddie said.

The tree limb bent.

"Just a little more," Freddie urged.

The cat took another step.

The branch bent even more.

"Almost there!" Freddie said.

Suddenly, there was a loud cracking sound.

Chipper gasped.

Darla shrieked.

"Oh, no!" Freddie cried.

Without warning, the branch broke, sending Freddie, Mr. Chewy, and the kite falling to the ground!

2

It happened so fast that there was nothing anyone could do about it.

One moment, Freddie and Mr. Chewy were clinging to a branch in a tree. The next moment, they were tumbling helplessly to the ground.

Freddie landed on his feet, but the branch knocked him to the ground. He was okay.

Mr. Chewy, however, wasn't so lucky. The branch knocked him sideways, and the cat landed right on his head!

"Mr. Chewy!" Darla shouted.

The cat got to his feet. He looked dizzy.

"Are you okay, buddy?" Freddie asked. He knelt down next to the cat. Mr. Chewy sat down, shook his head, and looked around. Thankfully, he wasn't hurt.

Freddie reached out and petted his cat on the head. "You're okay," he told Mr. Chewy. "You just bumped your noggin."

Mr. Chewy looked at Freddie. Then he scampered off.

Freddie stood and looked down at the broken branch on the ground. The kite's tail was still caught in it, but he was easily able to untangle it. When he was finished, he held the kite up.

"Wow!" Chipper said. "It's even bigger than I thought!"

"What are we going to do with it, Freddie?" Darla asked. "Are we going to fly it?"

"You bet!" Freddie said. "I'll bet it'll fly so high that it will reach the moon!"

"We'll need some new string," Chipper said.

"I have some at home," Darla offered, and she ran to her house.

"This is going to be a blast!" Freddie said. "Let's take it over to the park where there aren't any trees!"

Darla returned a few minutes later,

carrying a ball of string. "I don't think there is enough string to reach the moon," she said, "but we might be able to reach the clouds."

Freddie ran home to tell his mother that he was going to the park with Chipper and Darla. Mr. Chewy was sitting on the porch.

"Do you want to go to the park, Mr. Chewy?" Freddie asked.

The cat stood and chased after Freddie as he raced back to meet his friends.

"Let's go!" Freddie shouted to Chipper and Darla. Chipper and Freddie picked up the kite, and they held it carefully while they walked.

Soon, they reached the park. There

were only a few other kids playing on the swings. Otherwise, the park was empty.

And the wind was blowing strong.

"Here," Darla said, handing the ball of string to Freddie.

"Hang on to the kite," Freddie told Chipper, "so the wind doesn't carry it off."

While Chipper held the kite, Freddie carefully tied the string to it. He was careful to tie it good, too, so that it wouldn't untie while they were flying it.

"All set!" Freddie exclaimed.

"This is going to be fun!" Chipper said.

"Yeah," Darla said. "And we won't get into any trouble."

But Darla was wrong . . . because big trouble was only moments away.

About the author

Johnathan Rand is the author of the best-selling **'American Chillers'** and **'Michigan Chillers'** series, now with over 2,000,000 copies in print. In addition to the **'Chillers'** series, Rand is also the author of the **'Adventure Club'** series, including **'Ghost in the Graveyard' and 'Ghost in the Grand',** two collections of thrilling, original short stories. When Mr. Rand and his wife are not traveling to schools and book signings, they live in a small town in northern lower Michigan with their two dogs, Abby, and Lily Munster. He still writes all of his books in the wee hours of the morning, and still submits all manuscripts by mail. He is currently working on several projects, including the all-new **'Freddie Fernortner, Fearless First Grader'** series. His popular website features hundreds of photographs, stories, and art work. Visit:

www.americanchillers.com

Don't miss these exciting, action-packed books by Johnathan Rand:

Michigan Chillers (reading age 7-13)

#1: Mayhem on Mackinac Island
#2: Terror Stalks Traverse City
#3: Poltergeists of Petoskey
#4: Aliens Attack Alpena
#5: Gargoyles of Gaylord
#6: Strange Spirits of St. Ignace
#7: Kreepy Klowns of Kalamazoo
#8: Dinosaurs Destroy Detroit
#9: Sinister Spiders of Saginaw
#10: Mackinaw City Mummies

American Chillers: (reading age 7-13)

#1: The Michigan Mega-Monsters
#2: Ogres of Ohio
#3: Florida Fog Phantoms
#4: New York Ninjas
#5: Terrible Tractors of Texas
#6: Invisible Iguanas of Illinois
#7: Wisconsin Werewolves
#8: Minnesota Mall Mannequins
#9: Iron Insects Invade Indiana
#10: Missouri Madhouse
#11: Poisonous Pythons Paralyze Pennsylvania
#12: Dangerous Dolls of Delaware
#13: Virtual Vampires of Vermont
#14: Creepy Condors of California
#15: Nebraska Nightcrawlers
#16: Alien Androids Assault Arizona
#17: South Carolina Sea Creatures

Adventure Club series: (reading age 7-13)

#1: Ghost in the Graveyard
#2: Ghost in the Grand

www.americanchillers.com

AudioCraft Publishing, Inc.
PO Box 281
Topinabee Island, MI 49791

WATCH FOR MORE
FREDDIE FERNORTNER,
FEARLESS FIRST GRADER
BOOKS, COMING SOON!

Contents